# WHEN THE ELVES TOOK CHRISTMAS BACK

SANTA'S ROOM

This book is dedicated
to my daughter
Carmela

**First published in 2020 by Daniel Williamson**
**www.danielwilliamson.co.uk**
**This edition published in 2020**
**Text © Daniel Williamson 2020**
**Illustrations © Kleverton Monteiro 2020**
**Cover design © by Uzuri Designs 2020**

**ISBN 978-1-913583-18-7**

DW

**www.danielwilliamson.co.uk**

# WHEN THE ELVES TOOK CHRISTMAS BACK

WRITTEN BY
DANIEL WILLIAMSON

ILLUSTRATED BY
KLEVERTON MONTEIRO

When the snow starts to fall at the end of the year, we all know Christmas is coming.

Santa's workshop comes alive.

Working elves whistling and humming.

Every year, they all know the drill.
Each elf has a special task.
So why would the elves take Christmas back?
I'm ever so glad you asked...

The elves got busier every year.
Built huge machines to make toys.

Trying to keep up with all the demands
of good little girls and boys.

But the night before THIS Christmas eve,
Elf Tilly got such a shock.

She found a secret, hidden door,
chained up with a giant lock.

She took a hairpin from under her hat and used it as a pick.

She wiggled and twisted the pin until she heard the lock go click!

She took a
torch from
off the wall
and tiptoed
down and
through.

She simply
couldn't
believe
her eyes!

She saw
not one list,
but two!

Tilly needed a closer look.
She pulled them off
the shelves.

A true list
just for Santa's eyes

and a FAKE list
for the elves?!

The first list told a terrible truth.
'How could you Santa Claus?!'

Naughty list children
were getting gifts!

Completely
against elf laws!

When Santa Claus
went up to his room
the elves all gathered round.

Tilly made
a big announcement
and told them
what she'd found.

Head Elf Timeon called a meeting
while Santa Claus was sleeping.

They stood around the seeing snowball
and together they started peeping.

The children on earth were ever so rude. Talking back to their mums and dads.

Ignoring them whilst playing games on computers, phones and pads.

Leaving their clothes all over the floor.

Teasing their sisters and brothers.

Taking biscuits from the tin.

Not sharing their toys with others.

'You think that's bad, look at this!' said Webb.
'It's happened without us knowing.

The children on the naughty list!
Every year it's been growing and growing!'

'So what's the real numbers?'
How many good?
We need to know!' Said Jeff.

'That's just it! I can't believe it!
There's only 900 left!'

'He's clearly gone soft and forgotten our laws.
No more loading his sack!'

It's time for us to take a stand.
We're taking... Christmas... BACK!'

The elves snuck into Santa's room,
barely making a sound.

They tied up Santa and Mrs Claus
with tinsel all around!

The elves went out to the reindeer's barn and brought them all in from the cold.

They all sat round the big log fire, ate cookies and chocolates in gold.

When the sun came up on Christmas Eve
the elves had a brand-new plan.

They split up into different groups
and off they quickly ran.

Some took presents out of the sack.

Some polished up the sleigh.

The others brushed the reindeer's hides and fed them carrots and hay.

At 6pm the clock did chime.
'Action stations everyone!'

They pushed
the sleigh up
onto the ramp.

'This is going to be
such fun!'

Timeon sprinkled
the magic dust
on the reindeer's
antlers and feet.

'1,2,3!'
And they
whooshed
outside!

Into the
snow and
sleet.

One by one they delivered presents
to the GOOD little girls and boys.

To orphans and the poorest children,
who never get any toys.

Using elf magic,
they added some sparkle.
A fairy atop a new tree.

Baubles and glitter and candy canes too!
Exactly how Christmas should be.

With so few to visit they made it back quick.
They parked up Santa's sleigh.

And with sunrise approaching oh so fast
they prepared for Christmas Day.

But what about the naughty children,
whose day had started dawning?

Things turned out very different for them
on this frosty Christmas morning...

They ran downstairs,
jumping with joy.
Their hearts all filled with glee.

But not one Christmas
stocking was filled
and no presents
under the tree!

As more woke up the tears were flowing.
Every child on the naughty list sad.

'I'm sure we warned you this would happen
if your behaviour got too bad!

Children
being rude to
their parents,
Santa doesn't
want to hear.

To get on the
good list
you need to
be GOOD!

Still, better
luck next
year!'

And so it seemed the children would learn
that Christmas WILL be missed.

Unless they try much harder to
stay off the naughty list.

But what about the REST of the toys?
They were not wasted, no way!

They got to go to those who never
get to enjoy this day!

The reindeer and the elves alike,
made the workshop look so arty!

They turned the
music up

and
had...

...a Great Big Christmas Party!!!

# THE END

This author has also developed a bilingual book series designed to introduce children to a number of new languages from a very young age.

If you enjoyed reading this story, you will undoubtedly like other popular rhyming picture books from this author which are also currently available.

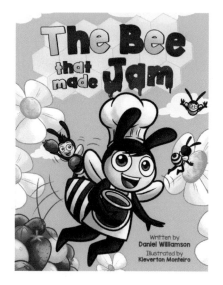

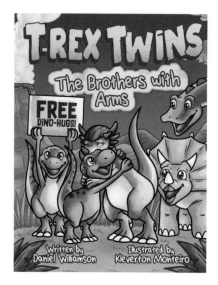

# A Message From The Author

I'd like to say a massive thank you to every single child and adult that read one of my books! My dream is to bring cultures together through fun illustrations, imagination and creativity via the power of books.

If you would like to join me on this journey, please visit my website danielwilliamson.co.uk where each email subscriber receives a free ebook to keep or we will happily send to a friend of your choice as a gift!

Nothing makes me happier than a review on the platform you purchased my book telling me where my readers are from! Also, please click on my links below and follow me to join my ever-growing online family! Remember there is no time like the present and the present is a gift!

Yours gratefully

## Daniel Williamson

@DanWAuthor

@danwauthor

@DanWAuthor

Printed in Poland
by Amazon Fulfillment
Poland Sp. z o.o., Wrocław